W9-AFL-002

WITHDRAWN

MR. NIGHTTIME
and the
DREAM MACHINE

based on a character created by DAVE NELSON

story by SUSAN SAUNDERS

illustrated by JEANETTE WINTER

SCHOLASTIC INC.

New York   Toronto   London   Auckland   Sydney

ISBN 0-590-33987-7

12 11 10 9 8 7 6 5 4 3 2 1   7 8 9/8 0 1 2/9
Printed in the U.S.A.   24

First Scholastic printing, May 1987

"It's time for bed," James's mother called down the hall.
"Aw, Mom," said James. "Do I have to?"

James hated to go to bed. When the light was off, he got the shivers and the creeps. If he lay there with his eyes open, he saw dark, scary things. But if he closed his eyes and fell asleep, it was much worse: a terrible nightmare would be waiting.

Slowly James put on his pajamas. He took as long as he could to brush his teeth: up and down, up and down. Finally, he climbed into bed.

James's mother read him his favorite story, about the adventures of a brave and handsome mouse. All too soon she reached the end.

"Read me another one?" asked James.

"Not tonight," said his mom. She tucked James's covers tight. "Sleep well," she said, giving him a kiss.

Then, with a click, she turned off the light.

"I don't like the light off," James said in a small voice.

"There's nothing to be afraid of," his mother told him. "Look at all the stars—you have thousands of tiny lights shining through your window. Good-night," she said. She closed the door.

James lay in his bed with the covers up to his chin. The room was dark. There were darker shadows in all the corners.

James stared out at the night sky. How many stars could he see? Maybe if he counted them, he wouldn't fall asleep, and the nightmare wouldn't come. James started to count: "One...two...three...four...."

Before he had counted even half the stars framed by his window, they suddenly disappeared! A thick, inky cloud billowed up to fill the whole sky. Then, out of the cloud rolled an enormous black engine with rumbling motors and shrieking wheels! As it rolled, it threw off blazing orange sparks.

A nightmare!

"I'll have to make the nightmare go away!" James told himself. "All I have to do is wake up."

James sat straight up in bed and rubbed his eyes. But the gleaming black engine was still rumbling toward him! James wasn't dreaming— it was real!

James tried to call out for his mother, but his mouth was too dry. He couldn't make a sound.

The horrible machine rolled toward his window—it looked big enough to squash the house! Now James could see someone driving it. It was a man wearing a big black hat. His eyes were mean and red, glinting out from under the brim. He was staring right at James!

James jerked the covers over his head and burrowed into his bed. He squeezed his eyes tightly shut. He stuffed his fingers in his ears.

Suddenly, James heard someone calling his name. What if the awful man in the black hat had come to get him?

"James. James—it's safe now." James still had his fingers in his ears, but he could hear the voice inside his own head. It wasn't a voice James recognized. But it was a kind, gentle voice.

James peered cautiously over the edge of his blanket. Standing next to him was a little old man with shining white hair. He seemed to glow in the dark, filling James's room with a warm, comforting light.

"Who are you?" James whispered.

"I'm Mr. Nighttime," the old man said. "Can you tell me what frightened you so badly?"

"I thought I was having a terrible dream," said James. "Suddenly the stars were gone, and there was a man in a black hat driving a huge, black engine right at my window! But it wasn't a dream. It was real!"

"Hmm," said Mr. Nighttime. "We'll have to do something about that."
He held out his hand. "Come along," he said to James.

James took Mr. Nighttime's hand. They stepped through
the bedroom window and flew into the night outside.

Mr. Nighttime looked up at the dark sky. He took a deep breath. *Whoosh!* He blew with all his might!

"The stars are back!" James cried.

"They were hidden behind a cloud of smoke," explained Mr. Nighttime. "It will be easy to find that scary engine — we'll just follow the smoke."

They didn't have far to go. The smoke had gathered in the valley beyond the next hill. Mr. Nighttime plunged into it, still holding James's hand.

The cloud of smoke was so thick they could hardly see. Inside there were horrible shrieks and rumbles, just like the ones James had heard from his bed. Then, out of the cloud, rolled the enormous, gleaming engine. On top of it sat the man in the black hat!

"Aha—Nighttime!" the man shouted gleefully. "You can't stop me this time! I've never been bigger or stronger!"

"Who is he?" James whispered, hanging back.

"Captain Racket," said Mr. Nighttime, "an old enemy of mine. He loves to scare children, and the more frightened children there are, the stronger he becomes."

"That's right—all the children are afraid of my new nightmare engine!"
Scaring children? Why, this guy was nothing more than a big bully.
Racket leaned menacingly toward James. "You're afraid, aren't you?"
he hissed.

Mr. Nighttime took James's hand in his.

"I am not afraid," James said, surprising himself.

"What's that you say?" snarled Captain Racket.

"I'm not afraid of you," said James.

Captain Racket shrank a little.

"That's it," murmured Mr. Nighttime, giving James's hand a little squeeze.

"I'm not afraid of you *or* your nightmare engine!" James said louder.
The captain was definitely shrinking!
"Again!" said Mr. Nighttime.

"I'll never be afraid of you again!" yelled James.

Now Racket was no larger than the mouse in James's
favorite story! "Nighttime—I'll get you for this!"
he squeaked. He slid down the side of the big black engine and
scuttled away.

    Mr. Nighttime reached into the engine. He twisted a knob. He turned a dial or two.

    The cloud of smoke disappeared. The clanking and shrieking stopped. Mr. Nighttime shifted a gear. The machine began to purr—like a cat, but a nice, fat, peaceful one.

Mr. Nighttime pushed some buttons. The machine made a sound like soft rain.

"I believe I'll call this my dream machine," Mr. Nighttime told James.
He waved his hand, and the dark engine turned suddenly light. It shone—
softly, like the stars. "From now on, there'll be only good dreams," he said.

Mr. Nighttime drove James home and tucked him into bed.
"Where are you going now?" James asked.
"I've got to get back to the stars," answered Mr. Nighttime. "My job is protecting the night. And now that I've got my dream machine....Well, sweet dreams," he said.

James drifted off to sleep to the sound of cats purring and the soft pattering of rain. And, that night, what he dreamed about was a kindly old man with shining white hair.